Cy Warman

The Prospector

Story of the Life of Nicholas C. Creede

Cy Warman

The Prospector
Story of the Life of Nicholas C. Creede

ISBN/EAN: 9783337077044

Printed in Europe, USA, Canada, Australia, Japan

Cover: Foto ©Raphael Reischuk / pixelio.de

More available books at **www.hansebooks.com**

THE

PROSPECTOR.

STORY OF THE LIFE OF
NICHOLAS C. CREEDE.

BY

CY WARMAN.

DENVER
THE GREAT DIVIDE PUBLISHING COMPANY
1894.

PREFACE.

The purpose of these pages is to tell the simple story of the life of an unpretentious man, and to show what the Prospector has endured and accomplished for the West.

THE AUTHOR.

THE PROSPECTOR.

CHAPTER I.

BIRTHPLACE — SCHOOL DAYS — BOY LIFE
ON THE FRONTIER—FAVORITE SPORTS.

FIFTY years and one ago, near Fort
Wayne, Indiana, Nicholas C. Creede,
the story of whose eventful life I shall
attempt to tell you, first saw the light
of day. When but four years old his
parents removed to the Territory of
Iowa, a country but thinly settled and
still in the grasp of hostile tribes
whose crimes, and the crimes of their
enemies, have reddened every river from
the Hudson to the Yosemite.

In those broad prairies, abounding

with buffalo and wild game of every
kind, began a career which, followed
for a half century, written down in a
modest way, will read like a romance.

When but a mere lad, young Creede
became proficient in the use of the
rifle and made for himself a lasting
reputation as a successful hunter. He
was known in the remote settlements as
the crack shot of the Territory, and being of a daring, fearless nature, spent
much of his time in the trackless forest and on the treeless plain.

As the years went by, a ceaseless
tide of immigration flowed in upon the
beautiful Territory until the locality
where the Creedes had their home was
thickly dotted with cabins and tents,
and fields of golden grain supplanted
the verdure of the virgin sod. As the
population increased, game became
scarce, and then, as the recognized

leader, young Creede, at the head of a band of boyish associates, penetrated the wilds far to the northward in pursuit of their favorite sport. On some of these hunting expeditions they pushed as far north as the British line, camping where game was abundant, until they had secured as much as their horses could carry back to the settlements.

This life in the western wilds awoke in the soul of the young hunter a love for adventure, and his whole career since that time has been characterized by a strong preference for the danger and excitement of frontier life.

The facilities for acquiring an education during young Creede's boyhood were extremely limited. A small school-house was erected about three miles from his home, and there the boys and girls of the settlement flocked

to study the simplest branches under a
male teacher, who, the boys said, was
"too handy with the gad." The boy
scout might have acquired more learn-
ing than he did, but he had heart
trouble. A little prairie flower bloomed
in life's way, and the young knight of
the plain paused to taste its perfume.
He had no fear of man or beast, but
when he looked into the liquid, love-
lit eyes of this prairie princess he was
always embarrassed. He had walked
and tried to talk with her, but the
words would stick in his throat and
choke him. At last he learned to
write and thought to woo her in an
easier way. One day she entered the
school-room, fresh and ruddy as the
rosy morn; her cherried lips made red-
der by the biting breeze ; and when
the eyes of the lass and the lover met,
all the pent-up passion and fettered

N. C. CREEDE.

affection flashed aflame from her heart
to his, and he wrote upon her slate:

" The honey bee for honey tips
    The rose upon the lea;
  Then how would be your honeyed lips
    If I could be the bee? "

The cold, calculating teacher saw
the fire that flashed from her heart to
her cheek, and he stepped to her desk.
She saw him coming and she spat
upon the slate and smote the sentiment
at one swift sweep. Then the teacher
stormed. He said the very fact that
she rubbed it out was equal to a con-
fession of guilt, and he "reckoned
he'd haf to flog her." A school-
mate of Creede's told this story to
me, and he said all the big boys held
their breath when the teacher went
for his whip, and young Creede sat
pale and impatient. "He'll never dare
to strike that pretty creature," they

thought; "she is so sweet, so gentle, and so good."

The trembling maiden was not so sure about that as she stepped to the whipping corner, shaking like an aspen. "Swish" went the switch, the pretty shoulders shrugged, and the young gallant saw two tears in his sweet-heart's eyes, and in a flash he stood between her and the teacher and said : "Strike me, you Ingin, and I'll strike you." "So'll I, so'll I," said a dozen voices, and the teacher laid down his hand.

CHAPTER II.

HIS FATHER'S DEATH — DRIFTING WEST
WARD — ADVENTURES ON THE MISSOURI.

DEATH came to the Creede family
when young Creede was but eight
years old. A few years later the youth
found a step-father in the family, and
they were never very good friends.
The boy's home-life was not what he
thought it should be, and he bade his
mother good-by and started forth to
face the world. In that thinly settled
country, the young man found it very
difficult to secure work of any kind,
and more than once he was forced to
fancy himself the "merry monarch of
the hay-mow," or a shepherd guarding
his father's flocks, as he lay down to
sleep in the cornfield and covered with

the stars. The men, for the most part,
he said, were gruff and harsh, but the
women everywhere were his friends,
and many a season of fasting was
shortened by reason of a gentle woman's sympathy and kindness of heart.
The brave boy battled with life's
storms alone; and when but eighteen
years old he set his face to the West.

Omaha was the one bright star in
the western horizon toward which the
eyes of restless humanity were turned,
and on the breast of the tide of immigration our young man reached the
uncouth capital of Nebraska. Perhaps
he had not read these unkind remarks
by the poet Saxe:

"Hast ever been to Omaha, where rolls the dark
        Missouri down,
    And forty horses scarce can draw an empty
        wagon through the town?
    If not, then list to what I say: You'll find it
        just as I have found it,

And if it lie upon your way, take my advice,
    and you'll go round it."

Omaha was then the great outfitting
point for the country to the westward,

Where everything was open wide,
And men drank absinthe on the side.

In the language of Field, "money
flowed like liquor," and a man who
was willing to work could find plenty
to do ; but the rush and bustle of the
busy, frontier town was not in keeping
with the taste of our hero, and he began to pine for the broad fields and
the open prairie. At first it was all
new and strangely interesting to him ;
and often, after his day's work was
done, he would wander about the town,
looking on at the gaming tables and
viewing the festivities in the concert
halls ; and when weary of the sights
and scenes, he would go forth into the

stilly night and walk the broad, smooth
streets till the moon went down. At
last he resolved to leave its busy
throng, and joining a party of wood-

choppers, he went away up the river
where the willows grew tall and slim.
He was busy on the banks of the sul-
len stream; he felt the breath of Spring
and the sunshine, and while the wild

birds sang in the willows, he wielded
the ax and was happy.

The wood was easily worked and
commanded a good price at Omaha,
and the young chopper soon found
that he was quite prosperous; was his
own master, and he whistled and
chopped while the she-deer fondled
her fawn and the pheasant fluttered
near him, friendly and unafraid. Once
a week the wood was loaded on a
"mackinaw" and floated down to the
city, where barges were always waiting, and where sharp competition often
sent prices way above the expectation
of the settlers.

One day, while making one of these
innocent and profitable trips down the
river, young Creede nearly lost his
life. For some reason, they were
trying to make a landing above the
city, and Creede was in the bow of

the boat, pulling a long sweep oar
fixed there on a wooden pin. While
exercising all his strength to turn the
boat shoreward in the stiff current, the
pin broke, he was thrown headlong
into the water and the boat drifted
above him. As often as he rose to
the surface, his head would strike the
bottom of the boat and he would be
forced down again. It seemed to him,
he said, that the boat was a mile
long and moving with snail-like speed.
He was finally rescued more dead
than alive, so full of muddy water
that they had to roll him over a
water-keg a long time before he could
be bailed out and brought back to
life.

When he reached Omaha and received his share of the cash from the
sale of the wood, he abandoned that

line of labor, and with the restlessness
of spirit and love for adventure which
has characterized his whole life, again
started westward.

The sturdy bull, with stately tread,
Submissive, silent, bows his head
And feels the yoke.   The creaking wain
Rolls leisurely across the plain:
Across the trackless, treeless land,
An undulating sea of sand,
Where mocking, sapless rivers run;
With swollen tongue and bloodshot eye,
Still on to where the shadows lie,
And onward toward the setting sun.

With weeping eyes he looks away
To where his free-born brothers play
Upon the plain, so wild and wide;
He turns his head from side to side,
He feels the bull-whip's cruel stroke;
Again he leans against the yoke.
At last his weary walk is done.
He pauses at the river's brink
And drinks the while his drivers drink.
Almost beside the setting sun.

CHAPTER III.

CREEDE'S arrival at the Pawnee Indian Reservation on the Loop fork of the Platte River marked an era in his eventful life. He began at this place a period of seven years' Indian fighting and scouting, which made him known in the valley of the Platte, and gave him a fame which would have been world-wide had he, like later border celebrities, sought for notoriety in print and courted the favor of writers of yellow covered literature.

Being naturally of a retiring, uncommunicative nature, he shrank from public attention; and no writer of fiction, or even a newspaper correspondent

29

could wrest from him a single point
on which to hang a sensational story.
While genial and sociable among his
associates on the trail, his lips were
locked when a correspondent was in
camp.

At that time the Union Pacific railway was in course of construction, and
hostile Indians continually harassed the
workers and did all in their power to
retard the progress of the work.
United States Cavalry troops were put
into the field to protect the working
corps, and workmen themselves were
provided with arms for their own defense. The Pawnee Indians were lying
quietly on their reservation, at peace
with the whites, never going forth except on periodical buffalo hunts, or on
the war-path against their hereditary
enemies, the Sioux.

Under these circumstances was begun

the building of a line across the plains. It was here that the now famous " Buffalo Bill " made his reputation as a buffalo killer, which has enabled him to travel around the world, giving exhibitions of life on the western wilds of America.

Mr. Frank North, then a resident of the Pawnee country, and thoroughly familiar with their language and customs, conceived the idea that the Pawnees would prove valuable allies to the regular troops in battling with the hostile Sioux, and with but little difficulty

secured governmental authority to enlist
two or three companies and officer
them with whites of his own choosing.
One of the very first men he hit upon
was Creede, whom he made a first lieutenant of one of the companies, a rela-
tive of the organizer being placed in
command with a captain's rank. This
man was a corpulent, easy-going fellow,
who sought the place for the pay.
There was nothing in his nature that
seemed to say to him that he should
go forth and do battle with the fearless hair-lifters of the plain. Even at
his worst, two men could hold him
when the fight was on. He was a very
sensible man, who preferred the quiet
of the camp and the government barber
to the prairie wilds and the irate red
man.

With Creede it was different. He
was young and ambitious, and having

been brought up by the firm hand of
a step-father, peace troubled his mind.
Nothing pleased him more than to have
the captain herd the horses while he
went out with his hand-painted Pawnees to chase the frescoed Sioux. He
set to work assiduously to learn the
language of the Pawnees and soon mas-
tered it. By his recklessness in battle
and remarkable bravery in every time
of danger, he gained the admiration
and confidence of the savage men, who
followed fearlessly where their leader
led. They looked upon Creede as
their commander, regarding the Captain
as a sort of camp fixture, not made
for field work, and many of their
achievements under their favorite leader
awoke amazement in their own breasts
and made them a terror to their Indian
foes. If there are those who think
these pages are printed to please

rather than from a desire to tell the
truth and do justice to a name long
neglected, I need but state that it
stands to-day as a prominent page of
the history of Indian warfare in the
West, that during their several years
of service, the Pawnee scouts were
never defeated in battle. The intrepid,
dashing spirit of their white leaders
inspired their savage natures with a
confidence in their own powers which
seemed to render them invincible.

Major North was himself a brave,
energetic officer, fearless in battle and
skilled in Indian craft, and not a few
of his appointments proved to be valuable ones from a fighting standpoint.
Because he was always with them,
sharing their danger and leading fearlessly when the fight was fierce, the
red scouts came to regard Lieutenant
Creede as the great "war chief"; and

E. DICKINSON.

never did they falter a moment when they were needed most by the Government. Every perilous expedition was intrusted to Creede and his invincibles. A favoritism was shown which permitted certain officers to remain in camp away from danger. They never knew how proud the Lieutenant was to lead his gallant scouts. It was a comparatively easy road to fame with so brave a band of warriors, and the attendant danger only served to appease the leader's appetite for adventures.

The notable incidents which marked Lieutenant Creede's career during his seven years' service as a scout would fill many volumes such as this. But a few can be touched upon; just enough to exhibit his fearless nature and his often reckless daring in the face of danger.

CHAPTER IV.

Hard down the plain the Red Man rode
Against the Red Man; Pawnee slew
His hated enemy, the Sioux,
And bathed him in his brother's blood.

For they were wily, wild and strong,
Revengeful, fearless, fierce and fleet.
They murmured: Oh, revenge is sweet
When Red Men ride to right a wrong.

LIEUTENANT MURIE—"GOOD INDIANS"—
"DON'T LET HER KNOW."

"READ to me, Jim," said the sweet girl-wife of Lieutenant Murie.

"I can't read long, my love," said the gallant scout. "I have just learned that there is trouble out West and I must away to the front. That beardless telegrapher, Dick, has been here with an order from Major North and they will run us out special at 11:30 to-night."

36

The Lieutenant picked up a collection of poems and read where he opened the book :

> " Tell me not, sweet, I am unkind,
>   That from the nunnery
>   Of thy chaste breast and quiet mind
>   To war and arms I flee."

"Oh, Jim," she broke in, " why don't they try to civilize these poor, hunted Indians ? Are they all so very bad ? Are there no good ones among them ?

"Yes," said the soldier, with a half smile. "They are all good except those that escape in battle."

"But tell me, love, how long will this Indian war last ? "

"As long as the Sioux hold out," said the soldier.

At eleven o'clock the young Lieutenant said good-by to his girl-wife and went away.

This was in the '60's. The scouts

were stationed near Julesburg, which
was then the terminus of the Union
Pacific track. The special engine and
car that brought Lieutenant Murie
from Omaha, arrived at noon, the
next day after its departure from the
banks of the muddy Missouri.

Murie had been married less than
six months. For many moons the
love-letters that came to camp from
his sweetheart's hand had been the
sunshine of his life, and now they
were married and all the days of
doubt and danger were passed.

An hour after the arrival of the
special, a scout came into camp to say
that a large band of hostile Sioux had
come down from the foot-hills and
were at that moment standing, as if
waiting—even inviting an attack, and
not a thousand yards away. If we
except the officers, the scouts were

nearly all Pawnee Indians, who, at the sight or scent of a Sioux, were as restless as caged tigers. They had made a treaty with this hostile tribe once, and were cruelly murdered by the Sioux. This crime was never forgotten, and when the Government asked the Pawnees to join the scouts they did so.

The scouts did not keep the warriors waiting long. In less than an hour, Lieutenant Murie was riding in the direction of the Sioux, with Lieutenant Creede second in command, followed by two hundred Pawnee scouts, who were spoiling for trouble. The Sioux, as usual, outnumbered the Government forces, but, as usual, the dash of the daring scouts was too much for the hostiles and they were forced from the field.

Early in the exercises, Murie and Creede were surrounded by a party of

Sioux and completely cut off from the
rest of the command. From these embarrassing environments they escaped
almost miraculously. All through the
fight, which lasted twenty minutes or

more, Creede noticed that Murie acted
very strangely. He would yell and
rave like a mad man—dashing here and
there, in the face of the greatest danger. At times he would battle single-
handed, with a half dozen of the

fiercest of the foe, and his very frenzy seemed to fill them with fear.

When the fight was over, Lieutenant Murie called Creede to him and said he had been shot in the leg. Hastily dismounting, the anxious scout pulled off the officer's boot, but could see no wound nor sign of blood. Others came up and told the Lieutenant that his leg was as good as new ; but he insisted that he was wounded and silently and sullenly pulled his boot on, mounted, and the little band of invincibles started for camp. The Pawnees began to sing their wild, weird songs of victory as they went along ; but they had proceeded only a short distance when Murie began to complain again, and again his boot was removed to show him that he was not hurt. Some of the party chaffed him for getting rattled over a little brush like that, and

again in silence he pulled on his boot
and they continued on to camp.

Dismounting, Murie limped to the
surgeon's tent, and some of his companions followed him, thinking to have a
good laugh when the doctor should say
it was all the result of imagination,
and that there was no wound at all.

When the surgeon had examined the
limb, he looked up at the face of the
soldier, which was a picture of pain,
and the bystanders could not account
for the look of tender sympathy and
pity in the doctor's eyes.

Can it be, thought Creede, that he is
really hurt and that I have failed to
find the wound? "Forgive me, Jim,"
he said, holding out his hand to the
sufferer, but the surgeon waved him
away.

"Why, you—you could n't help it,
Nick," said Murie. "You could n't

kill all of them; but we made it warm for them till I was shot. You won't let *her* know, will you?" he said, turning his eyes toward the medical man. "It would break her heart. Poor dear, how she cried and clung to me last night and begged me to stay with her and let the country die for itself awhile. Most wish I had now. Is it very bad, Doctor? Is the bone broken?"

"Oh no," said the surgeon. "It's only painful; you'll be better soon."

"Good! Don't let *her* know, will you?"

They laid him on a cot and he closed his eyes, whispering as he did so: "Don't let *her* know."

"Where is the hurt, Doctor?" Creede whispered.

"Here," said the surgeon, touching

his own forehead with his finger. "He is crazy—hopelessly insane."

All night they watched by his bed, and every few moments he would raise up suddenly, look anxiously around the tent, and say in a stage whisper: "Don't let *her* know."

A few days later they took him away. He was not to lead his brave scouts again. His reason failed to return. I never knew what became of his wife, but I have been told that she is still watching for the window of his brain to open up, when his absent soul will look out and see her waiting with the old-time love for him.

One of his old comrades called to see him at the asylum, a few years ago, and was recognized by the demented man. To him his wound was as painful as ever, and as he limped to his old friend, his face wore a look of

intense agony, while he repeated, just
as his comrades had heard him repeat
an `hundred times, this from Swinburne:

> "Oh, bitterness of things too sweet,
>   Oh, broken singing of the dove.
> Love's wings are over-fleet,
> And like the panther's feet
>   The feet of Love."

"Good-by, Jim," said the visitor, with
tears in his voice.

"Good-by," said Jim. Then glancing
about, he came closer and whispered :
"Don't let *her* know."

It is a quarter of a century since
Murie lost his reason and was locked
up in a mad-house, and these years
have wrought wondrous changes. The
little projected line across the plain has
become one of the great railway sys-
tems of the earth. "Dick," the beardless
operator who gave Murie his orders
at Omaha, is now General Manager

Dickinson. The delicate and spare
youth, who wore a Winchester and red
light at the rear end of the special, is
now General Superintendent Deuel, and
Creede, poor fellow, he would give
half of his millions to be able to
brush the mysteries from Murie's mind.

CHAPTER V.

HAD N. C. Creede remained a poor prospector all his days, these pages would never have been printed. That is a cold, hard statement; but it is true. Shortly after the fickle Goddess of Fortune sat up a flirtation with the patient prospector, the writer met with a gentleman who had served on the plains with the man of whom you are reading, and he told some interesting stories. We became very well acquainted and my interest in the hunter, scout, prospector and miner increased with every new tale told by his companion on the plains. Those who know this silent man of the mountains are well aware of his inborn modesty and

47

of the reticence he manifests when ques-
tioned about his own personal experiences. Hence, the writer as well as the
reader must rely largely upon the stories told by his old comrade, the first
of which was this :

A large body of Sioux Indians were
camped near North Platte, Nebraska,
having come there to meet some peace
commissioners sent out from Washington. We were camped about eight
miles below them, quietly resting during the cessation of hostilities, yet constantly on the alert to guard against a
foray from our foes above. The Sioux
and the Pawnees were bitter enemies,
constantly at war with each other, and
as we knew they were aware of the
existence of our camp, we feared some
of them might run down and endeavor
to capture our stock. Our best scouts
were sent out every evening in the di-

rection of North Platte to note any
evidences of a night raid that might
appear, and our Indians were instructed
to have their arms in perfect order and
in easy reach when they rolled up in
their blankets for sleep.

Creede's horse had become lame and
was next to useless for field work. We
did not have an extra animal in camp,
and for three or four days he tried
hard to trade the crippled horse to an
Indian scout for a good one. He offered extravagant odds for a trade, but
the Indians knew too well the near
proximity of a natural enemy and
would take no risks on being without
a mount should trouble come.

We were sitting in the tent one evening, taking a good-night smoke, when
some one began to chaff Creede about
his "three-legged horse." Nick took it
all good-naturedly, smiling in his own

quiet way at our remarks, and soon he
sat with his eyes bent on the ground,
as if in deep reflection. Suddenly he
arose, buckled on his pistols, picked up
his rifle and started from the tent without a word.

"Where are you going, Nick?" some
one asked.

"Going to see that the pickets are
out all right," he replied, as the tent
flap closed behind him.

This seemed natural enough, and we
soon turned into our blankets and
thought no more of the matter. When
we rolled out at daybreak next morning, it was noticed that Creede's blankets had not been used and that he
was not in the tent. One of the boys
remarked that he had lain down out in
the grass to sleep and would put in an
appearance at breakfast time, and we all
accepted this as the true explanation of

his absence. Half an hour later, when
we were about to eat breakfast, one of
the pickets came in and reported something coming from up the river. Our
field-glasses soon demonstrated the fact

that it was a man riding one horse and
leading four others. As he came closer,
we recognized Creede, and he soon rode
in, dismounted and began to uncinch
his saddle, with the quiet remark :

"Guess I ought to get one good mount out of this bunch."

"Where did you get them?" Major North asked.

"Up the river a little ways."

"How did you get up there? Walk?"

"Not much I did n't. I rode my lame horse."

"What did you do with your own horse?"

"Traded him for these even up."

He had gone alone in the night, stolen into the herd of the Sioux near North Platte, unsaddled his lame horse and placed the saddle on an Indian's, and, leading four others, got away unobserved and reached camp safely. It was a bold and desperate undertaking, but one entirely in keeping with his adventurous spirit.

CHAPTER VI.

DURING the summer of '68, a large
party of Pawnee Indians, men and
squaws, left the reservation on the Loop
fork for a buffalo hunt in the country
lying between the Platte and Republican Rivers. These semi-annual hunts
were events of great interest to the
tribe, for by them they not only secured supplies of meat, but also large
numbers of robes, which were tanned by
the squaws and disposed of to traders
for flour and groceries, and for any
other goods which might strike the Indian fancy.

At this time the Pawnee scouts were
lying in camp on Wood River, about a

mile from the Union Pacific Railroad
station of that name. The hostile
Indians had for some weeks made no
aggressive demonstration, and our duties
were scarcely sufficient to edge up the
dull monotony of camp life. Once a
week about half of the company would
be sent on a scout to the west along
the railway, two days' march, four days
of the week being consumed by these
expeditions.

Half of the company had gone on this
weekly scout, leaving but one white officer in camp, Lieutenant Creede. He
had, if I recollect aright, but eighteen
men fit for duty, a number of others
being disabled by wounds received in
recent battles. The second day after the
hunting party left, the section men from
the west came into Wood River Station
on their hand-car, and excitedly reported
that a band of about fifty Sioux had

crossed the track near them, headed
south. Joe Adams was the agent at
Wood River, and he at once sent a
messenger to the Pawnee camp to tell
Lieutenant Creede of the presence of
the hostiles. Creede hastily mounted
his handful of warriors, and in less than
twenty minutes was dashing forward on
the trail of the Sioux. The time consumed by the section men in running
into the station, a distance of about four
miles, and the consequent delay caused
by sending the news to Creede, and the
catching up and saddling of the ponies
had given the Sioux a good start, and
when the scouts had reached the Platte
the hostiles had crossed over and were
concealed from view in the sand-hills
beyond.

Crossing the wide stream with all possible haste, the game little ponies, strug-
gling with the treacherous quicksand for

which that historic river is noted, the
scouts struck the trail on the opposite
bank and pushed rapidly forward.
Although they knew that the Sioux
outnumbered them three to one, the
Pawnees were eager for the fray—an
eagerness shared in by their intrepid
commander. Chanting their war-songs,
their keen eyes scanning the country
ahead from the summit of each sand-
hill, they pushed onward with the
remorseless persistence of blood-hounds
up the trail of fleeing fugitives.

About three miles from the river, on
reaching the top of a sand-hill, the enemy was discovered a mile ahead, moving carelessly along, oblivious of the fact
that they were being pursued. Concealed by the crest of the hill, the
Pawnees halted to view the situation,
and Lieutenant Creede covered the hostiles with his field-glass. An impreca-

tion came from his lips as he studied
the scene in front, and crying out a
sentence in the Pawnee tongue, his warriors crowded about him. His experienced eye had shown him that they
were Yankton Indians, then at peace
with the whites. He took in the situation in a moment. They had learned
of the departure of the Pawnee village
on a buffalo hunt, and were after them
to stampede and capture their horses,
kill all of their hated enemy they could
and escape back to their reservation.

All this he told to his warriors, and
the field-glass in the hands of various
members of the party corroborated the
fact that, as United States scouts, they
had no right to molest the Yankton
bands. The impetuous warriors chafed
like caged lions, and demanded in vigor-
ous terms that the chase should be re-
sumed. One cool-headed old man, a

chief of some importance in the tribe, addressed Lieutenant Creede substan- tially as follows :

"Father ; you are a white man, an officer under the great war chief at Washington, and you would rouse his anger by battling with Indians not at war with him and his soldiers. We are Pawnee Indians, and the men yonder are our hated foes. They go to attack our people, to kill our fathers, sons, brothers, the squaws and children, and steal their horses. It is our duty to protect our people. It is not your duty to help us. Go back, father, to our camp, and we, not as soldiers, but as Indians, will push on to the defense of our people. Listen to the words of wis- dom and go back."

The situation was a trying one. The Lieutenant well knew that if he led his scouts against the Yanktons he would

have to face serious trouble at Washington and meet with severe censure
from General Augur, then commanding
the Department of the Platte. He realized that his official position would be
endangered, and that he might even
subject himself to arrest and trial in
the United States Courts for his action.
For some moments he stood with his eyes
bent upon the ground in deep reflection, the Indians eying him keenly and
almost breathlessly awaiting his reply.
It was a tableau, thrilling, well worthy
the brush of a painter. The hideously
painted faces of the Indians scowling
with rage ; their blazing, eager eyes re-
flecting the spirit of impatience which
swayed their savage souls ; the hardy,
faithful ponies cropping at the scant
grass which had pierced the sand ; the
Lieutenant standing as immovable as
a rock, his face betraying no trace of

excitement, calmly, silently gazing at the
ground, carefully weighing the responsi-
bilities resting upon him,—all went to
make up a picture so intensely thrilling
that the mind can scarcely grasp its
wild features.

When the Lieutenant spoke, he did so
quietly and calmly. There was a light
in his eyes which boded no good to the
pursued, but his voice betrayed not the
least excitement. He said :

" For several years I have been with
you—have been one of you. We have
often met the enemy in unequal numbers, but we have never been defeated.
In all the battles in which I have led
you, you never deserted me. Should I
desert you now ? I know that I will
be censured, perhaps punished, but those
Yanktons shall never harm your people.
I will lead you against them as I would
against a hostile band, and on me will

rest all the responsibility. We go now as Pawnee Indians, not as United States scouts, and go to fight for our people. Mount!"

Grunts of satisfaction greeted his words. They would have been followed by wild yells of savage delight had there been no fear of such a demonstration disclosing their presence to the Yanktons. Horses were quickly mounted, and the band again took the trail with an impatience which could scarcely be curbed.

The Yanktons were soon again sighted, and the scouts adopted the Indian tactics of stealing upon their foes. Skirting the bases of sand-hills, keeping from sight in low grounds and following the bed of gulches, they pressed on, until the enemy was discovered less than three-fourths of a

mile ahead, and yet unconscious of the
presence of a foe.

Halting in a low spot in the hills,
the Pawnees hastily unsaddled their
ponies and stripped for the fight. Indians invariably go into a battle on
bareback horses, as saddles impede the
speed of the animals in quick movements. When again mounted, the Lieutenant gave the command to advance.
On reaching the crest of a sand-hill,
the Pawnees discovered their enemy
just gaining the summit of the next,
about five hundred yards distant. The
Yanktons discovered their pursuers at
the same moment, and great commo-
tion was observed in their ranks. They
hastily formed themselves for battle,
and then one of them who could speak
English, cried out :

"Who are you, and what do you
want ?"

"We are Pawnee Indians, and we want to know where you are going," Creede shouted in reply.

"You are Pawnee scouts, and are soldiers of the United States. We are Yankton Sioux at peace with the Government, and you cannot molest us."

"You are moving against the Pawnee village, now on a buffalo hunt," Creede replied. "You want to kill our people and steal their horses. We are Pawnee Indians, and are here to fight for our people. If you take the trail back across the Platte, we will not disturb you, but if you attempt to move forward, we will fight you. Decide quick!"

The leaders of the Yankton band gathered about the interpreter in council, while Creede interpreted what had been said to his warriors. It was with difficulty he could restrain them

from dashing forward to the attack.
In a few moments the Yankton interpreter shouted :

" If you attack us, the Government
will punish you and reward us for
our loss. We do not fear you as
Pawnees, but we are at peace and do
not want to fight you because you are
soldiers of the great father at Washington. We are many and you are
few, and we could soon kill you all,
or drive you back to your camp. Go
away and let us alone."

" You are the enemy of our people, and you go to kill them," the
Lieutenant replied. " We will fight
for them, not as soldiers, but as Pawnees. You must make a move now,
instantly. We will wait but a minute.
If you take the back trail, it will be
good. If you move forward, we will
make you halt and go back."

The only reply was a command from the Yankton leader to his followers, in obedience to which they started forward in their original direction. Creede shouted a command to his men, and with wild yells they dashed down the slope and up the side of the hill on which their enemy had last been seen. On a level flat beyond the hill, the Yanktons were found hastily forming for battle, and with tiger-like impetuosity, the scouts dashed forward, firing as they advanced.

The wild dash of the Pawnees seemed to bewilder the Yanktons, and they were thrown into confusion. They quickly rallied, however, and for fully an half-hour they fought desperately. The mad impetuosity of the Pawnee again threw them into confusion, and scattering like frightened sheep, they fled from the field. The Pawnees pursued them, and a running fight was maintained over several miles of country. The Yanktons were at last so scattered that they could make no show of resistance, and with all possible speed sought the river crossing and fled toward their agency. It was afterwards learned that they sustained a loss of eight killed and quite a large number wounded. The Pawnees lost but one man killed, but many were wounded on the field. Several horses were killed. Creede's army blouse was riddled with bullets and arrows.

Returning from the field, "Bob White," a Pawnee, reached Wood River in advance of the scouts, and by making motions as of a man falling from a horse, and repeating the word, "Lieutenant," created the impression that Creede had been killed, and the agent

AMETHYST MINE.

telegraphed the news to Omaha, where
it was published in the daily papers.
When the scouts reached the station,
however, the gallant Lieutenant was at
their head. When he dismounted, it
was observed that he limped painfully,
and in explanation said, that in one of
the charges his horse had fallen upon
him, severely bruising and spraining
one of his legs. This was what "Bob"
had tried to tell, but the agent interpreted his signs to mean that the intrepid leader had been killed in battle.

When the Yanktons reached their
agency, they reported that while quietly
moving across the country, the Pawnee
scouts, being in the service of the United
States, had attacked them in overwhelm-
ing numbers and driven them back to
their reservation. The matter was laid
before the authorities at Washington,
referred to General Augur, and by him

to Major North, who was already in
possession of Creede's explanation of the
affair. Considerable red-tape correspond-
ence followed, and as the Yanktons
were off their reservation without permission, and in direct violation of
orders, the matter was allowed to drop.
Creede was doubly a hero in the eyes
of his scouts after this episode, and
when the Pawnee village returned, and
it was learned how the Lieutenant had
battled in their behalf, they bestowed
upon him the most marked expressions
of gratitude and adoration.

CHAPTER VII.

ONE of the most daring acts in the history of this daring man was committed in Western Nebraska in 1866. From boyhood days, he had been noted as a hunter, and during the years which he spent in the scouting service, his splendid marksmanship and extraordinary achievements in the pursuit of game earned for him the reputation of being the best hunter west of the Missouri River. His success in that line was phenomenal and elicited expressions of surprise from all who had a knowledge of his work, and from those who were told of it.

Killing buffalo was not regarded by
Creede, or by any of the hunters, as the
best evidence of skill in marksmanship
or in hunting. Any one who could ride
a horse and fire a rifle or revolver
could kill those clumsy, shaggy animals
much easier than they could pursue and
kill the ordinary steers on the western
ranges to-day. In fact, the range steer
is a far more dangerous animal when
enraged than was the buffalo, for it
possesses greater activity, and is more
fleet of foot. The men who have
gained notoriety on account of the
number of buffalo they have killed are
looked upon with quiet contempt by
the true hunters of the plains and
mountains, who justly claim that hunting excellence can only be shown in the
still hunt, where tact and skill are re-
quired to approach within shooting distance of the elk, deer or antelope, and

proficient marksmanship is necessary to kill it. When buffalo were plenty on the western plains, it was not at all unusual for women to ride after and kill them, and incur little, if any, risk of personal danger. Miss Emma Woodruff, a school teacher on Wood River in the sixties, and who afterwards married a telegraph operator at Wood River Station, became quite noted as a buffalo hunter, and regarded it but as an ordinary achievement to mount her pony and kill one of the shaggy monsters. The long-haired showmen who infest the country and tell thrilling stories of their desperate adventures and narrow escapes while hunting the buffalo, draw largely upon their imagination for bait to throw out to the gullible. No one in a dozen of them ever reached the west bank of the Missouri River. Every frontier man will agree that the

so-called scouts, cowboys and Indian
fighters who pose in dime museums,
dime novels or behind theatrical foot-
lights, are in nearly every instance the
most shameless frauds, whose long hair
and unlimited "gall" make them heroes
in unexperienced eyes. Since the death
of Kit Carson, but one long-haired man
has earned a reputation as a scout, and
while he was once, for a brief season,
allured into the dramatic business, and
now gives platform entertainments when
his duties will permit him to do so, he
is not a showman, but is yet in Government employ. He is a trusted secret
agent of the Department of Justice, and
is engaged in a calling almost as dangerous as was his scouting service—that
of running down the desperate men
who are engaged in selling liquor to
Indians. Long hair is the exception
and not the rule among scouts, and a

cowboy who permits his locks to cluster
over his shoulders is laughed at by his
fellow knights of the saddle and classed
as a crank.

You shall read this story as it fell
from Creede's own lips when I pressed
him to tell it to me. It was this incident which first gained from him the
full confidence and unstinted admiration of the Indian scouts:

"Game, through some cause, was very
scarce near our camp, and one day I
saddled my favorite horse and rode
southward, determined to get meat of
some kind before returning. I went
about fifteen miles from camp, and
after hunting some four or five hours
without success, made up my mind the
game had all left the country. I started
to return by a circuitous route, desiring
to cover as large a scope of country as
possible, and get some meat if it was

at all to be found. After traveling
perhaps an hour through the sand-hills,
I came upon a fresh trail of pony
tracks, and I knew the tracks were
made by Indian ponies, and hostile
Indians, too, for none of our scouts
were away from camp. I determined
to follow the trail and ascertain if the
ponies all bore riders, and, if possible,
to get close enough unobserved to see
from the appearance of the Indians who
they were, and if it was a hunting or
war party. They were headed in the
direction in which I desired to go, and
after tightening up my saddle cinches
and looking to see if my pistols were
in order, I took the trail. I judged
from the trail that there were about
twenty-five or thirty Indians in the
party, and I soon learned that my esti-
mate was a nearly correct one.

"When I reached the top of the first

little hill ahead of me, I came in full view of the party not more than a quarter of a mile distant. They saw me at the same time, as I knew from the confusion in their ranks. I tell you, in a case of that kind, one wants to do some quick thinking, and if ever a man jogged his brain for a scheme to get out of an ugly scrape, I did right then and there. If I tried to run, I knew they would scatter and get me, and in less time than it takes me to tell it, I had made my plan and started to put

it into execution. I saw that my only
chance, though a desperate one, would
be to make them believe I was ahead
of a party in their pursuit, and
taking off my hat, I made frantic
motions to the rear, as if hurrying up
a body of troops, and then, putting
spurs to my horse, dashed right toward
them, and when close enough, began
firing at them with my rifle. The
scheme worked beautifully, for without
firing a shot, they seemed to become
terror-stricken and fled on through the
hills. The course lay through low sand-
hills which often concealed them from
view, but I pressed on, firing at every
chance. I chased them for fully three
miles ; two of them died and I captured
three ponies which fell behind, and then
left the trail and made for camp. I
found it hard to make the scouts believe my story, and some of them quite

plainly hinted that I had found the
ponies in the hills and had seen no
Indians. I saw at once that they
doubted me, and determined to convince them of the truth of what I had
told them. The next morning I took a
dozen or more of them and went back
to the scene of the chase, and we were
not long in finding all the coyotes had
left of the two bodies.

" That affair firmly established my
reputation with the scouts, and ever
after they fully relied on my judgment
as a war chief. Through all our future
operations, they trusted me implicitly,
and would follow me any place I chose
to lead them."

CHAPTER VIII.

WHEN NEW FLOWERS BLOOM ON THE
GRAVES OF OTHER ROSES — PLUNKETY
PLUNK OF UNSHOD FEET — HE HAD
RECKONED WELL.

IN the early springtime, at that time
of the year when all the world grows
glad ; when the green grass springs
from the cold, brown earth ; when new
flowers bloom on the graves of other
roses ; when every animal, man, bird and
beast, each to his own kind turns with
a look of love and tender sympathy,
we find the restless Red Men of the
Plains on the war-path.

One day at sunset, Lieutenant Creede
rode out from Ogallala, where the scouts
were stationed, guarding the railway
builders. It was customary for some

one to take a look about at the close
of day, to see if any stray Sioux
were prowling around. About six miles
from camp, he came to a clump of
trees covering a half dozen acres of
ground. Through this grove the scout
rode, thinking perhaps an elk or deer
might be seen ; but nothing worth
shooting was sighted, till suddenly he
found himself at the farther edge of the
wood and on the banks of the Platte.
Looking across the stream, he saw a
small band of hostile Sioux riding in
the direction of the river, and not more
than a mile away. His field-glasses
showed him that there were seven of
the Sioux, and without the aid of that
instrument, he could see that they had
a majority of six over his party. They
were riding slowly in the direction of
the camp. Creede concluded that they
intended to cross over, kill the guards,

and capture the Government horses.
His first thought was to ride back to
camp, keeping the clump of trees between him and the Indians, and
arrange a reception for the Sioux.

The river was half a mile wide and
three feet deep. Horses can't travel
very rapidly in three feet of water.

In a short time they had reached the
water's edge and the scout could hardly
resist the temptation to await their
approach, dash out, take a shot at
them, and then return to camp. That
was dangerous, he thought ; for, if he
got one, there would still be a half a
dozen bullets to dodge. A better plan
would be to leave his horse in the
grove, crawl out to the bank, lie concealed in the grass until the enemy was
within sixty yards of him, then stand
up and work his Winchester. The first
shot would surprise them. They would

all look at their falling friend ; the
second would show them where he was,
and the third shot would leave but
four Indians. By the time they swung
their rifles up another would have
passed to the Happy Land, and one
man on shore, with his rifle working,
was as good as three frightened Indians
in the middle of the river.

Thus reasoned the scout, and he
crept to the shore of the stream. He
had no time to lose, as the Indian
ponies had finished drinking and were
already on the move.

As the sound of the sinking feet of
the horses grew louder, the hunter was
obliged to own a feeling of regret. If
he could have gotten back to his horse
without them seeing him, he thought
it would be as well to return to
camp and receive the visitors there.
Just once he lifted his head above the

grass, and then he saw how useless it
would be to attempt to fly, for the
Indians were but a little more than a
hundred yards away. Realizing that
he was in for it, he made up his
mind to remain in the grass until the
Sioux were so near that it would be
impossible to miss them. Nearer and
nearer sounded the plunkety-plunk of
the unshod feet of the little horses in
the shallow stream, till at last they
seemed to be in short-rifle range, and
the trained hunter sprang to his feet.
He had reckoned well, for the Indians
were not over sixty yards away, riding
tandem. Creede's rifle echoed in the
little grove ; the lead leaped out and
the head Indian pitched forward into
the river. The riderless horse stopped
short. The rifle cracked again, and
the second Red Man rolled slowly
from the saddle ; so slowly that he

barely got out of the way in time to
permit the next brave, who was almost
directly behind him, to get killed when
it was his turn. The remaining four
Indians, instead of returning the fire,
sat still and stone-like, so terrified
were they that they never raised a
hand. Two more seconds ; two more
shots from the trusty rifle of the scout
and two more Indians went down, head
first, into the stream. Panic-stricken,
the other two dropped into the river
and began to swim down stream with
all their might. They kept an eye on
the scout and at the flash of his gun
they ducked their heads and the ball
bounded away over the still water.
Soon they were beyond the reach of
the rifle. Returning to their own side
of the river, they crept away in the
twilight, and the ever sad and thought-
ful scout stood still by the silent

stream, watching the little red pools of blood on the broad bosom of the slowly running river.

Three of the abandoned bronchos turned back. Four crossed over to Creede and were taken to camp.

The two sad and lonely Sioux had gone but a short distance from the river, when one of them fell fainting and soon bled to death. He had been wounded by a bullet which had passed through one of his companions who was killed in the stream. ·The remaining Indian was afterwards captured in battle and he told this story to his captors, just as it was told to the writer by the man who risked his life so fearlessly in the service of Uncle Sam.

CHAPTER IX.

SIT-TA-RE-KIT SCALPED ALIVE — AN IN-
DIAN NEVER CARES TO LIVE AFTER HE
HAS LOST HIS SCALP.

DURING the month of May, 1865,
the scouts were given permission
to go with the Pawnees on their annual
buffalo hunt. The Pawnees were greatly
pleased, for where there are buffaloes
there are Indians; and the Sioux were
ever on the lookout for an opportunity
to drop in on the Pawnees when they
were least expected. Late one after-
noon a party, eight in number, of the
scouts became separated from the main
force during the excitement incident to
a chase after buffaloes; and, before they
had the slightest hint of danger, were
completely surrounded by a band of at

least two hundred Sioux. The hunters
were in a small basin in the sand-hills
while the low bluffs fairly bristled with
feathers. The Sioux would dash forward, shoot, and then retreat. Lieutenant Creede, two other white men and
five Pawnees composed the party of
scouts. This little band formed a circle
of their horses, but at the first charge
of the savage Sioux, the poor animals
sank to the sand and died. The scouts
now crouched by the dead horses, and
half a dozen Sioux fell during the next
charge. One savage who appeared to
be more fearless than the rest, dashed
forward, evidently intending to ride
over the little band of scouts. Alas
for him! there were besides the Lieutenant, three sure shots in that little circle,
and before this daring brave had gotten
within fifty yards of the horse-works, a
bullet pierced his brain. Instead of

dropping to the ground and dying as
most men do, this Indian began to leap
and bound about, exactly like a chicken
with its head cut off, never stopping
until he rolled down within fifteen feet
of the scouts.

There was a boy in Creede's party,
Sit-ta-re-kit by name, a very intelligent
Pawnee, eighteen years old, who had
gone with the Lieutenant to Washington to see the President of the United
States. There seemed to be no shadow
of hope for the scouts ; and this young
man started to run. Inasmuch as he
started in the direction of the camp,
which was but a mile away, it is but
fair to suggest that he may have taken
this fatal step with the hope of notify-
ing the Pawnees of the state of affairs.
This was the opinion of Lieutenant
Creede ; while others thought he was
driven wild by the desperate surround-

ings. He had gone less than a hundred yards when a Sioux rode up beside him and felled him to the ground with a war club. The young scout started to rise, was on his knees, when

the Sioux, having dismounted, reached for the scout's hair with his left hand. All this was seen by the boy's companions.

"Oh, it was awful!" said Creede, relating this story to the writer. "We had been together so much. He was

so brave, so honest and so good. Of
course, he was only an Indian; but I
had learned to love him, and when I
saw the steel blade glistening in the
setting sun—saw the savage at one
swift stroke sever the scalp from that
brave boy's head, I was sick at heart."
After he had been scalped, the boy got
up and walked on, right by the savage
Sioux. He was safe enough now.
Nothing on earth would tempt an Indian to touch a man who had been
scalped, not even to kill him.

A Pawnee squaw was working in the
field one day when a Sioux came down
and scalped her. She knew if she returned to her people she would be
killed. It was not fashionable to keep
short-haired women about; and, in her
desperate condition, she wandered back
to the agency. The agent was sorry
for her and he took her in and cured

her head and sent her back to her people. But they killed her; she had
been scalped.

But let us return to the little band
in the basin surrounded by the Sioux.
It is indeed a small band now. Four
of them are dead, one scalped and gone ;
but as often as their Winchesters bark,
a Sioux drops. There was nothing left
for them now but to fight on to the
end.

Death in this way was better than
being burned alive. There was no
hope—not a shadow; for, how were
they to know that one of their companions had seen the Sioux surround
them and that the whole force of Pawnee scouts were riding to the relief of
this handful of men, who were amusing
themselves at rifle practice while they
waited for death.

With a wild yell, they dashed down

upon the murderous Sioux, and, without firing a shot, they fled from the field, leaving thirteen unlucky Indians upon the battle ground.

The brave boy never returned. He took his own life, perhaps; for an Indian never cares to live after he has lost his scalp, knowing that his companions look upon him as they look upon the dead.

CHAPTER X.

N C. CREEDE, the Prince of Prospectors and new-made millionaire, is one of the gentlest men I have ever met, notwithstanding most of his life has been spent in scenes not conducive to gentleness. His friendship is loyal and lasting; and he is as true to a trust as the sunflower is to the sun. Although a daring scout and fearless Indian fighter, he is as tender and sympathic as the hero of the "*Light of Asia*."

Creede and I were traveling by the same train one day, when he asked me if I knew a certain soldier-man—a Captain Somebody; and I said, " No."

93

"I raised my rifle to kill him one
day and an Indian saved his life," said
he, musingly.

I looked at the sad face of my companion in great surprise. I could
hardly believe him capable of taking a
human life, and I asked him to tell me
the story.

"It was in '65, I believe," he began.
"We had just captured a village on a
tributary of the Yellowstone, and were
returning to our quarters on Pole
Creek. Just before going into camp,
we came upon five stray Sioux, who
had been hunting and were returning
to their camp on foot. Two of the
Sioux were killed and three captured.
On the following morning, General
Augur, who was in command, gave
orders to my Captain to take thirty
picked scouts and go on an exploring
trip, and to take the three captives

with us, giving special orders to see
that none of the prisoners escaped.

"When everything was in readiness,
the three Sioux were brought out and
placed on unsaddled ponies, with their
hands tied behind them. Not a word
could they utter that we could understand; but O, the mute pleading and
silent prayers of those poor captives!
It was a dreary April morning; the
clouds hung low and the very heavens
seemed ready to weep for the poor,
helpless Indians.

"I don't know why they did, but
every few moments, as we rode slowly
and silently across the dank plain, they
would turn their sad eyes to me, so
full of voiceless pleading that I found
it was impossible to hold my peace
longer. Riding up to the side of the
Captain, I asked him what he intended
to do with the captives. 'Wait and

you will see,' was his answer. 'What,' said I, 'you don't mean to kill them? That would be cold-blooded murder.' 'I'll see that they don't get away,' said the cruel Captain. I thought if he would only give them a show, and suggested that we let them go two hundred yards, untie their hands and tell them to fly; but to this proposition he made no reply. Then we went on silently, the poor captives riding with bowed heads, dreaming daydreams, no doubt, of leafy arboles and running streams; of the herds of buffalo that were bounding away o'er the distant plain.

"The scouts were all Pawnees, and their hatred for the Sioux dated from the breaking of a treaty by the latter, some time previous. After the treaty had been completed, the two tribes started on a buffalo hunt. When they

arrived at the Republican River, and
the Pawnees had partly crossed, and
the rest were in the stream, the Sioux
opened fire upon them and slew them
without mercy. The Pawnee were divided into three bands by this treacherous slaughter and never got together
afterward. The bitterest hatred existed
between the two tribes, and the Government was using one to suppress the
other.

"The three captives would never have
surrendered to the Pawnees had they
not seen the white men, to whom they
looked for mercy. How unworthy they
were of this confidence, we shall soon
see.

"The Pawnees were by no means
merciful. I have heard them tell often,
how they skinned a man alive at Raw-
hide, a little stream in Nebraska, with
all the gruesome and blood-curdling

gestures. The white man, the victim of the skinners, had made a threat that he would kill the first Indian he saw. It happened to be a squaw; but the man kept his word. His rifle cracked and the squaw dropped dead. The train had gone but a few miles when the Indians overtook the wagons and forced them to return to the scene of the shooting, where they formed a circle, led the victim to the center, and actually skinned him alive, while his companions were compelled to look on."

I agreed that all this was interesting; but insisted upon hearing the story of the cruel Captain and the captives.

"Oh, yes," said the prospector. "Well, I had dropped back a few feet, two of the naked Indians were riding in front of the Captain, when he lifted his pistol; it cracked and I saw a little

red spot in the bare back of one of
the bound captives. His fettered arms
raised slightly; his head went back,
and he dropped from the horse, dead.
The pistol cracked again: Another little

red spot showed up between the shoulders of the other Indian. I felt the
hot blood rush to my face, and impul-
sively raised my rifle—mechanically, as
the natural helper of the oppressed—
when a Pawnee, who was riding at my

side, reached out, grasped my gun, and said, 'No shoot 'im.'

"The third captive, who was riding behind with the Indian scouts, attempted to escape, seeing how his companions were being murdered, but was killed by the guard.

"The Captain dismounted and scalped the two victims with a dull pocket-knife, and afterward told how they rolled up their eyes and looked at him like a dying calf.

"I could tell you more; but when I think of that murder, it makes me sick at heart, and I can see that awful scene enacted again."

CHAPTER XI.

MR. CREEDE'S success is due largely
to his lasting love for the mountains, which was love at first sight. It
was in 1862 that the scouts were
ordered to Dakota; and it was then he
saw for the first time the grand old
Rockies. They were nearing the Big
Horn Range, and the sight of snow in
August was something the Indians of
the plains could not understand. In
fact, they insisted that it was not snow,
but white earth, and offered to stake
their savings on the proposition. Some
of them were foolish enough to bet
their ponies that there was no snow on
the ground in summer time. Late that

evening they camped at the foot of the range, and on the following morning, four men were sent up to investigate and decide the bets. The result was a change of horses, in which the Indians got the worst of the bargain. For nearly a week they lingered in the shadows of the cooling mountains and were loth to leave them.

When, some years later, the scouts
were mustered out of service, Creede
returned to his old home in Iowa. But
he soon tired of the dull, prosy life
they led there ; and, remembering the
scent of wild flowers and the balmy
breeze that blew down the cool cañons
of the Big Horn Mountains, he determined to return to the region of the
Rockies. Already he had seen his
share of service, it would seem. For
more than a dozen years he had slept
where night had found him, with no
place he could call his home ; and yet
there are still a dozen years of doubt
and danger through which he must
pass. For him the trail that leads to
fortune and fame, is a long one ; and
many camps must be made between his
pallet on the plains and his mansion
by the sea. The path of the prospector, like that of the poet, lies in a

stony way, and nothing is truer than the declaration that :

> The road is rough and rocky,—
>   The road that leads to fame;
> The way is strewn with skeletons
>   Of those who have grown lame
> And have fallen by the wayside.
>   The world will pass you by,
> Nor pause to read your manuscript
>   Till you go off and die.

CHAPTER XII.

THE life of a prospector is one
fraught with hardships and priva-
tions and, in locations infested by Indians, often one of peril. But in his
search for the precious metals, the
hardy prospector gives but little
thought to personal danger. With his
bedding, tools and provisions, packed
upon the backs of trusty little burros,
he turns from the haunts of men and
plunges into the trackless wilds of the
mountains. Guided by the star of hope,
he pursues his ceaseless explorations in
the face of hardships which would
appall any heart not buoyed up by a
keen expectation of "striking it rich"

in the near future, and springing at one bound from poverty to wealth.

Of the great army of prospectors constantly seeking to unearth the vast treasure hidden in the rocky breast of the mountain ranges of the West, few attain a realization of the hopes which lead them onward, and secure the wealth for which they so persistently toil. The instances are very rare in which the prospector has reaped an adequate reward for his discoveries. In the great majority of cases where really valuable leads have been located, the discoverers, not possessing the capital necessary to develop them, have accepted the first offer for their purchase, and have sold for a mere song properties which have brought millions to those who secured them. The most notable instance in the annals of mining in the West, where fortune has

rewarded the prospector for his labors,
is that in which figures Mr. N. C.
Creede. His is a life tinged with romance from boyhood to the present
time. This story may serve as an in-
centive to less fortunate prospectors to
push onward with renewed hopes; for
in the great mountain ranges of the
West, untold riches yet lie hidden from
the eye of man.

The register at the Drover's Hotel,
Pueblo, if it had a register, held the
name of N. C. Creede, some time in the
fall of 1870. He marveled much at the
Mexicans. For years he had lived
among the Indians and was well acquainted with many tribes; but this
dark, sad-faced man, was a new sort of
Red Skin.

Pueblo in '70, was not the city we
see there to-day. It was a dreary cluster of adobe houses, built about a big

cotton-wood tree on the banks of a
poor little river that went creeping
away toward the plain, pausing in
every pool to rest, having run all the
way from Tennessee Pass over a rocky
road through the Royal Gorge.

Less than thirty summers had
brought their bloom to him, but he
felt old. Life was long and the seven
years of hard service on the plains had
made him a sad and silent man. So
much of sorrow, so much of suffering
had he seen that he seldom smiled and
was much alone. Away from his old
companions, a stranger in a strange land,
he looked away to the snow-capped
crest of the Sangre de Christo and
said: "There will I go and find my
fortune." Then he remembered he was
poor. But he was young, strong and
willing to work, and he soon found
employment with Mr. Robert Grant,

who was very kind to this lone man in
many ways. For six months he labored
and looked away to the mountains,
whose stony vaults held a fortune and
fame for him. In the spring of 1871,
the amateur prospector went away to
the hills and spent the summer hunting, fishing and looking for quartz.
After this, life away from the grand
old mountains was not the life for him.
Here was his habitation. This should
be his home.

CHAPTER XIII.

FRUITLESS SEARCHES—MET A STREAK OF HARD LUCK—BUT LATER HE STOOD ON THE SUN-KISSED SUMMIT.

THE winter of 1871–2 was spent at Del Norte, and in the following spring Creede, with a party of prospectors, went to Elizabethtown, New Mexico. This town was a new one, but was attracting considerable attention as a placer field. Like a great many other mining camps, the place was overdone, and unless a man had money to live on, the outlook was not very cheerful. Finding no work to do the young prospector staked a placer claim and commenced operations single-handed and alone, and the end of the third day, cleaned up and found himself in pos-

session of nine dollars' worth of gold
dust. This gave him new courage. He
worked all the summer; but when winter came on, he discovered that after
paying his living expenses which are
always lofty in a new camp, he had
only made fair wages; the most he
had made in a single day was nine
dollars.

The winter following found the prospector in Pueblo again, working for
another stake, this time in the employ
of Mr. George Gilbert. Early in the
spring of 1873, he took the trail.
Upon this occasion, he found his way
to Rosita in Custer County where the
famous Bassick Mine was afterward discovered, and within a few miles of Silver Cliff, which was destined to attract
the attention of so many prospectors,
bringing into the mining world so
much shadow and so little shine.

From Rosita he went to the San Juan district and prospected for several months, returned to the east side of the range, and finally made a second trip to the San Juan, but found nothing worth the assessment work.

About this time the Gunnison country began to attract attention and with other fortune-seekers Creede went there. This trip, like all his prospecting tours west of the "Great Divide" panned poorly. Never did he make a discovery of importance on the western slope, and now he made a trip to Leadville. Here he met with a well-defined streak of hard luck. After hunting in vain for a fortune, he was taken with pneumonia, lingered for a long time between life and death, but finally recovered. If Creede had died then, he would have received, probably, four lines in the *Herald*, which would have

been to the effect that a prospector had
died of pneumonia in his cabin at the
head of California Gulch, and had been
dead some time when discovered, as
the corpse was cold and the fire out.
He was of no great importance at that
time, but since then he has marched
from Monarch to the banks of the Rio
Grande, leaving a silver trail behind
him, until at last, standing on the sun-
kissed summit of Bachelor mountain,
he can look back along the trail and
see the camp-fires that he lighted with
tired hands, trembling in the cold,
burning brightly where the waste
places have been made glad by the
building of hundreds of happy homes.

Creede has labored long and faith-
fully for what he has, never shrinking
from the task the gods seem to have
set before him. Almost from his in-
fancy he has been compelled to do

battle with the world alone, and the writer is proud of the privilege of telling the story of his life, giving credit where credit is due, and putting the stamp of perfidity upon the band of stool-pigeons who have camped on his trail for the purpose of claiming credit for what he did.

CHAPTER XIV.

FOREST fires started by the Indians,
carelessly or out of pure deviltry,
had swept the hills to the east of the
divide in Chaffee County, and sufficient
time had elapsed to allow a pompadour
of pine to grow in the crest of the
continent, so thick that it was almost
impenetrable. In July, 1878, having
chopped a trail through this forest,
Creede came to the head of the little
stream where the prosperous town of
Monarch now stands. For thirteen days
the prospector was there alone, not a
soul nearer than Poncha Springs, fifteen
or twenty miles away.

Elk, deer and bear were there in abundance, and the prospector had little difficulty in supplying himself with fresh meat. In fact, the bear were most too convenient,—they insisted upon coming in and dining with the silver-seeker.

Creede located a claim, called it the Monarch, and gave the same name to the camp. Among the first claims located was one called the "Little Charm." It proved to be a good property — but not till it had passed into other hands. The formation in the Monarch district was limestone, and in limestone the prospector never knows what he has. To-day he may be in pay ore and to-morrow pick it all out. Creede had picked out some promising prospects in the same formation. He had discovered the Madonna, but had more than he could handle. He

took Smith and Gray up there and
told them where to dig; they dug
and located the Madonna claim.
They kept it and worked the
assessments for five years
and then sold it to Eylers
of Pueblo for
sixty thousand
dollars.

AMETHYST TRAMWAY.

The ore is very low grade, but was of great value to these men, who were smelters, for the lead it carried.

By the time the snow began to fall there were a number of prospectors in the new camp, and having tired of the place, which was one of the hardest, roughest regions in the state, Creede sold what claims he had for one thousand seven hundred dollars, but returned every summer for five years, cleaning up in all about three thousand dollars.

In Monarch, as in his last success, there were a number of jealous miners who wanted the name of the camp changed.

They were, or most of them, at least, light-weight politicians, who did n't care a cent what the town was called so long as they had the honor of naming it, but the name was never changed.

CHAPTER XV.

LEAVING Monarch, the prospector
journeyed through Poncha Pass, over
into the San Luis Valley, and began to
climb the hills behind the Sangre de
Christo range. On a little stream called
Silver Creek he made a number of locations, among them the Bonanza, and he
called the new camp by that name, just
as he named Monarch after what he
considered his best claim. The country
here was more accessible and conse-
quently a more desirable field for prospecting. South of Bonanza, Creede
located the "Twin Mines," which proved
to be good property. The ore in the

118

twin claims carried two ounces of gold to the ton.

A year later when the pioneer prospector decided to pull out and seek new fields, he was able to realize fifteen thousand dollars in good, hard-earned money. One claim was sold for two thousand dollars, the money to be deposited in Raynolds' bank at Salida; but the purchasers for some reason insisted that the money be deposited in a Poncha bank, very little known at that time, but whose president shortly afterward killed his man and became well, but not favorably, known. Creede's two thousand dollars went to the banker's lawyers. The bank closed, and now you may see the ex-president in a little mountain town pleading at the bar—not the bar of justice.

The camp has never astonished the mining world, but it has furnished employment for a number of people, and that is good and shows that the West and the whole world is richer and better because of the discoveries of Creede.

Creede now determined to see a little, and learn something of mining in other sections of the West. Leaving Colorado, he traveled through Utah, Nevada, Arizona and California, prospecting and studying the formation of the country in the different mining camps. The knowledge gained on this trip proved valuable to the prospector in after years. This was his school. The wide West was his school-house, and Nature was his teacher.

CHAPTER XVI.

A BEAR STORY—THE BEAST INFURIATED —A NEW DANGER CONFRONTS HIM.

AN old prospecting partner of Mr. Creede's told the following story to the writer, after the discovery of the Amethyst, which lifted the discoverer into prominence, gave him fame and a bank account—and gave every adventuress who heard of his fortune, a new field :

A man by the name of Chester, Creede and I were prospecting in San Miguel County, Colorado, in the 80's. We had our camp in a narrow cañon by a little mountain stream. It was summer time ; the berries were ripe, and bear were as thick as sheep in New Mexico. About sunset one evening

I called Creede out to show him a cow which I had discovered on a steep hillside near our cabin.

The moment the Captain saw the animal he said in a stage whisper : " Bear ! " I thought he was endeavoring to frighten me ; but he soon convinced me that he was in earnest.

Without taking his eyes from the animal, he spoke again in the same stage whisper, instructing me to hasten and bring Chester with a couple of rifles. When I returned with the shooting irons I gave the one I carried to Creede, who instructed me to climb upon a sharp rock that stood up like a church spire in the bottom of the cañon. From my high place I was to signal the sharp-shooters, keeping them posted as to the movements of the bear.

" You come with me," said Creede to the man who stood at his side. It

occurred to me now for the first time
that there was some danger attached to
this sport. I could n't help wondering
what would become of me in case the
bear got the best of my two partners.

If the bear captured them and got
possession of the only two guns in the
camp, my position on that rock would
become embarrassing, if not actually
dangerous. I turned to look at Chester, who did not seem to start when
Creede did. Poor fellow, he was as
pale as a ghost. "See here," he said,
addressing the man who was looking
back, smiling and beckoning him on as
he led the way down toward the noisy
little creek which they must cross to
get in rifle range of the bear, "I'm a
man of a family, an' don't see why I
should run headlong into a fight with a
grizzly bear. I suppose if I was a single man, I would do as you do; but

when I think of my poor wife and
dear little children, it makes me home-
sick." Creede kept smiling and beckoning with his forefinger. I laughed
at Chester for being so scared. He
finally followed, after asking me to look
after his family in case he failed to
return. Just as a man would who was
on his way to the Tower.

Having reached the summit of the
rock, I was surprised to see the big
bear coming down the hill, headed for
the spot where the hunters stood coun-
seling as to how they should proceed.
I tried to shout a warning to them, but
the creek made such a fuss falling over
the rocks that they were unable to hear
me.

A moment more and she hove in
sight, coming down the slope on a long
gallop. Probably no man living ever
had such an entertainment as I was

about to witness. In New York ten
thousand people would pay a hundred
dollars a seat to see it; but there was
no time to bill the country—the curtain
was up and the show was on. Creede,
who was the first to see the animal,
shot one swift glance at his companion,
raised his rifle, a Marlin repeater, and
fired. The great beast shook her head,
snorted, increased her pace and bore
down upon her assailants. Again and
again Creede's rifle rang out upon the
evening air, and hearing no report from
Chester's gun, he turned, and to his
horror, saw his companion, rifle in hand,
running for camp. Many a man would
have wasted a shot on the deserter, but
Creede was too busy with the bear, even
if he had been so inclined. Less than
forty feet separated the combatants
when Creede turned, and at the next
shot I was pleased to see the infuriated

animal drop and roll upon the ground.
In another second she was up again,
and she looked more like a ball of
blood than an animal. Now she stood
up for the final struggle. I saw Creede
take deliberate aim at her breast. He
fired and she fell. I shouted with joy
as I thought she must be dead now,
but was surprised to see that Creede
was still shooting. As rapidly as I
clapped my hands his rifle shouted, and
he put four more great leaden missiles
into the body of the bear.

With that unaccountable strength that
comes to man and beast in the last
great struggle, the mad monster stood
up again. Nothing on earth or under
the earth could be more awful in appearance than was this animal. One
eye had been forced from the socket,
and stood out like a great ball of fire.
Blood fairly gushed from her open

mouth, and the coarse, gurgling, strangling sound that came from the flooded throat, was so awful that it fairly chilled the blood in my veins. For a second she stood still and glared at her adversary as if she would rest or get a breath before springing upon him.

Again I saw the hunter take deliberate aim. This time he aimed at the open mouth, the ball crashed up through the brain and the bear dropped dead.

I did not shout now. This was the third time I had seen him kill that same bear, and I expected her to get up again. Creede was not quite satisfied, for I saw him hastily filling his magazine; and it was well.

The hunter stepped up to the great dead animal and placed his feet upon her, as hunters are wont to do, when another danger confronted him.

Attracted by the shooting and the coarse cries of the wounded bear, her mate came bounding down the slope to her rescue.

The first act had been interesting, but I confess that I was glad when the curtain dropped. Creede was tired. Even

an experienced hunter could hardly be
expected to go through such a perform·
ance without experiencing some anxiety.
I almost held my breath as the big
animal bore down upon the tired
hunter. Nearer and nearer he came,
and Creede had not even raised his rifle
to his shoulder. Now the bear was less
than twenty feet away and Creede stood
still as a statue with one foot resting
on the body of the dead.

I was so excited that I shouted to
him to shoot, but he never knew it;
and if he had, it would have made no
difference.

At last the bear stopped within eight
feet of the hunter, and bear-like, stood
up. Now the rifle was leveled and it
seemed to me it would never go, but
it did. The big bullet broke the bear's
neck, and he fell down dead at the
hunter's feet.

CHAPTER XVII.

IN 1886 at Monarch, George L.
Smith, Charles H. Abbott and N. C.
Creede formed a company for prospecting purposes. Smith and Abbott were
to furnish the funds, while Creede did
the searching. This company lasted for
nearly four years, during which time a
number of locations were made, some of
which they could have sold at a good
profit ; but they held on for more
money, always spending liberally for
the development of their property.

Just before the little company went
to pieces, Smith and Abbott went over
in the mountains to where Creede with
two miners had worked all winter, on

Spring Creek. After making a thorough examination of the prospects, it was agreed that they should abandon the hole and break up the partnership. This action was not taken because of any disagreement; but the men who were putting up the money were discouraged.

Just before visiting the property, Smith and Abbott received a letter from Creede, in which he said:

"I notice by the general tone of your letters lately, that you are both becoming discouraged with my hard luck. I assure you that I am doing the best I can. Take new courage, stay with me a little longer, and I shall find the greatest silver mine in America. I feel it in my bones."

But they had tried so long and spent so much money, that they had become discouraged.

Smith, since that time has made a
small fortune out of mines. Senator
Abbott, who is well known and uni-
versally respected, is the manager of a
Monarch property in which he is
largely interested. He has a home in
Denver where his family live ; but
spends most of his time in the mountains, still toiling, and hoping that he,
too, may find a fortune in the hoary
hills.

CHAPTER XVIII.

THE HOLY MOSES—ELIJAH WAS AWKWARD AND HARD TO SPELL—WAGON WHEEL GAP.

SHORTLY after the abandonment of the claim on Spring Creek, and the withdrawal of Senator Abbott from the company, Smith and Creede went over to the head of West Willow. They believed that at that point they could find an extension of the vein they had been working, and Creede believes to this day that they did. Here they located a claim. They were not working together that day and Creede was alone when the location was made. Many are the stories that have been told as to how the first mine in the now famous camp of Creede got its name, none of which are within a mile of the truth.

Having driven a stake, Creede sat
down to think of a name. There was
little or nothing in a name, he thought,
but he wanted to please his partner.

He remembered that Smith had named
three claims in Monarch, the "Madonna," the "Cherubim," and the "Ser-
aphim," and he would follow in that
line. Creede was not well versed in

Biblical history, so knew very little of the saints and angels. He looked above where the eagle flew by the ragged rocks and thought of Elijah; how he hid away in the hills, and how the ravens came down and fed him. He looked at his torn and tattered trousers, and thought of Lazarus. Neither of these names pleased him. Lazarus suggested poverty and Elijah was awkward and hard to spell. He looked away to the stream below, where the willows were, and thought of the babe in the bulrushes. He looked at the thick forest of pine that shaded the gentle slopes, and thought of the man who walked in the wilderness. And he called the mine the Moses; then fearing that his partner might object even to that, rubbed it out, and wrote " Holy Moses."

The story of the new strike spread like a prairie fire, and soon found its

way to the ears of Mr. D. H. Moffat,
then president of the Denver & Rio
Grande Railroad Company, who was
always on the lookout for a good mine.
One day in the early autumn of 1890,
Mr. Moffat, with a party of friends, in-
cluding Mr. Eb Smith, his mining ex-
pert, and Capt. L. E. Campbell, then
quartermaster at Fort Logan, set out in
the president's private car for Wagon
Wheel Gap, which was at that time
the terminus of the track. Captain
Campbell had turned the traffic of the
post to the "Scenic Line" and in a little while a warm friendship sprang up
between him and the railway management, the result of which has proved
very beneficial to all concerned.

Arriving at Wagon Wheel Gap, the
party set out in stages for the Holy
Moses, a distance of ten miles. The
road lay along the grassy banks of the

Rio Grande, one of the prettiest streams in the West. A ride through such a beautiful country could not be tiresome, and before they began to feel the fatigue of the journey, they reached the claim.

It took but a short time to convince the speculators that the Moses was good property, and before leaving, a bond was secured at seventy thousand dollars. Returning to Denver, the property was divided. Mr. Moffat took one half, the other half being divided between Captain Campbell, Mr. Eb Smith, Mr. S. T. Smith, who was then general manager of the Denver & Rio Grande Railroad Company, and Mr. Walter S. Cheesman, at that time a director, each paying in proportion to what he got. Most of the men interested in this new venture were very busy, and they were at a loss to know what to do for a reliable man to manage the property. About that time Captain Campbell secured a year's leave of absence from the army and took up his residence at the new camp. A comfortable cottage was built in the beautiful valley, just where the West Willow pours her crystal flood into the Rio Grande, and here the Campbells had their home. Mrs. Campbell, who is a niece of Mrs. General Grant, had lived many years in Washington, but she appeared as much at home in Creede camp as she did in the Capital.

CHAPTER XIX.

Here's a land where all are equal,
Of high and lowly birth;
A land where men make millions
Dug from the dreary earth.
Here the meek and mild-eyed burros
On mineral mountains feed,
It's day all day in the day-time,
And there is no night in Creede.

The cliffs are solid silver,
With wondrous wealth untold;
And the beds of the running rivers
Are lined with purest gold.
While the world is filled with sorrow
And hearts must break and bleed,
It's day all day in the day-time,
And there is no night in Creede.

CREEDE CAMP—THE NEW FIELD—INCOR-
PORATION OF THE AMETHYST.

AS manager of the Holy Moses, Captain Campbell employed Mr. Creede,
in whom he had implicit confidence, to
prospect, on a salary, with the under-

standing that the prospector should
have one third of what was found.
Creede had a world of faith in the
country, and had imparted this confidence to the Captain.

An ordinary mortal would have been
satisfied with thirty-five thousand dollars, but Creede's dream had not yet
been realized. The prophecy made in
his last letter to his old partners had
not been fulfilled. He had now enough
to keep him when old age should
come upon him, and laying his little
fortune aside for a rainy day, he
started out with the intention of wast-
ing his grub-stake, his salary and his
time.

As if he would lose all trace of the
Moses vein, he passed over a low divide
and began to toil up the steep, densely-
wooded side of Bachelor Mountain.
How many miles this man had walked

in the wilds of the mountains, alone with Nature and Nature's God ! The frosts of fifty winters have touched his face and there are streaks of gray in his soft, thin hair. At his heels is the faithful dog. He, too, has seen his share of service, and is as gray as his master.

The mountain gets its name from the Bachelor mine which was one of the first discoveries. This claim was located by a Mr. Bennett in the year, 1885. Mr. John Herrick, a jolly bachelor of Denver, formerly of New York, had been pounding away in this claim for several years ; but not until the mountain had given up millions to others, did he wrest a fortune from her rugged breast.

Slowly up the mountain-side the lone prospector worked his way. Some float was found and traced along through

the heavy forest. Now and then the
great roots of the pine trees forced
some rich looking rock to the surface,
and the prospector was tempted to stop
and dig, but the float kept cropping
out. There was mineral in that mountain and he would follow the outcrop-
ping until it disappeared.

Already the prospector began to
dream day-dreams of fortune and fame.
Slowly up the mountain he toiled, finding fresh signs of wealth at every step.
Once in a while the temptation to stop
was so great, that it was almost irre-
sistible ; but still he went on. When
half-way up the long slope, the out-
croppings disappeared and he turned
back. His trained eye soon led them
to the proper place and before the sun
went down that day, Creede had laid
the foundation for the fortune of not
less than a half dozen people.

The new find was called the Amethyst, and upon this vein are located now the Last Chance, New York Chance, the Bachelor and a number of other valuable claims that are worth, or will be when silver is remonetized. from one to five million dollars apiece.

In May, 1892, the Amethyst Mining Company was incorporated.

Mr. D. H. Moffat was elected president; N. C. Creede, vice-president;

MR. ALLENBY,
Foreman of the Amethyst.

Walter S. Cheesman, secretary and treasurer, and Captain L. E. Campbell, general manager. A tramway was built to carry the ore from the mine to the Denver & Rio Grande Railroad Company's track, which cost the Amethyst company many thousands of dollars. Splendid shaft and ore houses were built at the mine, making almost a little city where Creede had walked through a wilderness of pines. The Last Chance, adjoining the Amethyst, owned by Senator E. O. Wolcott, and others, spent a fortune in development work; but the mine has yielded millions to its owners. To Mr. Jacob Sanders of Leadville is due the credit for having organized the Last Chance Mining Company, one of the strongest in the camp.

When the news of the incorporation of the Amethyst Mining Company went out to the world, many inquiries were made by brokers for stock; but none was ever offered for sale.

The capital stock, five million dollars, is divided as follows; Mr. Creede owns one third, Mr. Moffat one third, Captain Campbell one sixth, Mr. S. T. Smith and Mr. Cheesman, a twelfth each. When the statement is made that this mine for some time paid a monthly dividend of ninety thousand dollars, it is easy to figure the daily income of any or all of the gentlemen interested in the property. What a striking example for the monometallist who argues that silver can be produced at a profit at the present prices; but it stands as a well-known fact, that, taking the whole output of Creede camp from the date of the discovery of the Amethyst vein to the present time, every ounce of silver that has gone down the Rio Grande has cost the producers more than a dollar.

Of the army of prospectors who lose themselves in the hills every spring, nothing is ever heard, except of the very few who find a fortune. Among the gambling dens in a mining camp, the scores of men who lose from one to one thousand dollars every night keep their own secret; but let one man win a hundred, and you will hear the barber tell the city marshal that "Redy Quartz broke de bank at Banigan's las' night, too easy." Mining and prospecting are only legitimate gambling, and it is the tens of thousands of little losers that keep the game going.

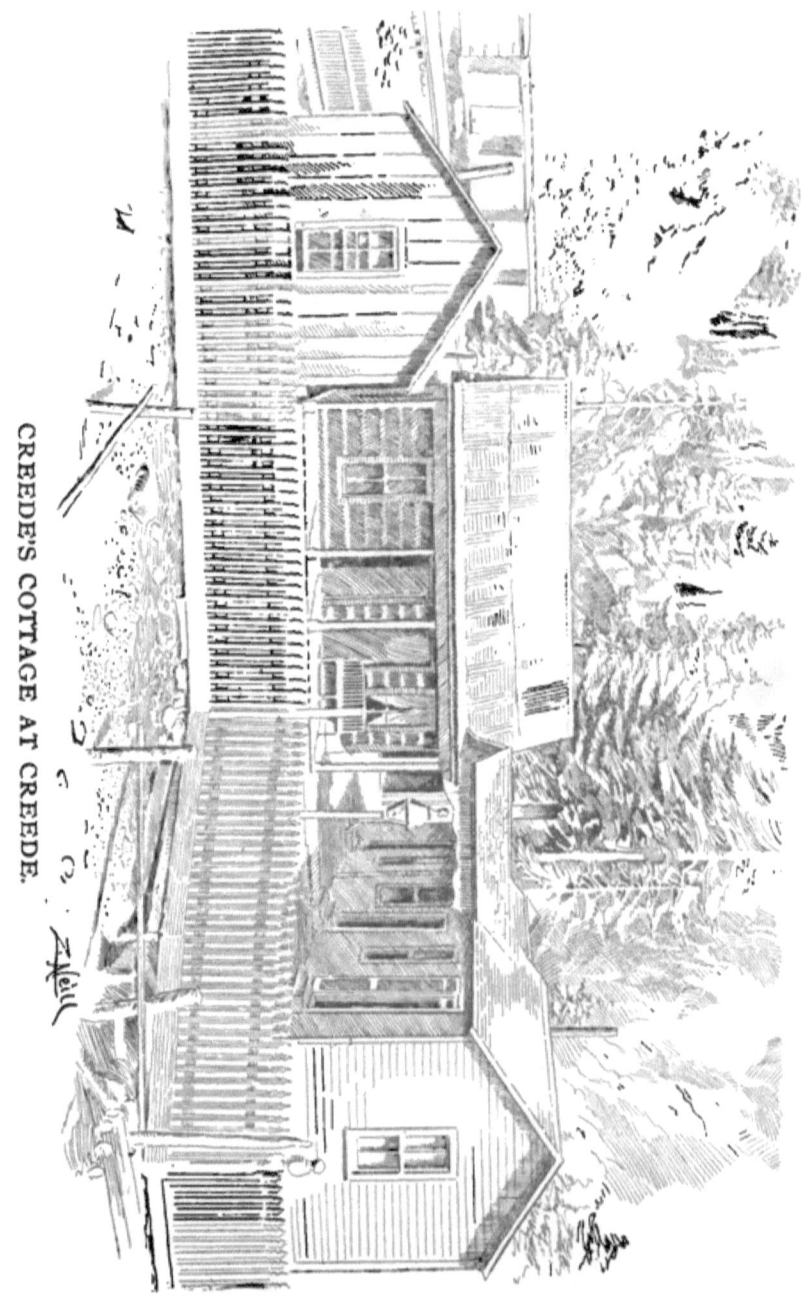

CREEDE'S COTTAGE AT CREEDE.

CHAPTER XX.

AWAY in the hills, far above the
bluebells, where the day dawned
early and the sunlight lingered when
the day was done, the lone prospector
had his home. At times he would have
a prospecting partner; but often for
months he lived alone in the hills, with
no companion save his faithful dog, who
for thirteen years followed silently
where his master led. One day while
talking of his past experiences, the prospector said: "When I try to taste
again the joy that was mine when I
first learned that I was a millionaire,
I am disappointed. Like Mark Twain's
dime, it could be enjoyed but once.

147

Great joys, like great sorrows, are soon
forgotten ; but there are things that
are as fresh in my memory as if these
years had been but
moments. I shall
never forget

the many beautiful spots where my
little dog and I have camped — always on the sunny south hills where
the sun coaxed the grass to grow and
the flowers to blow, often, it seemed, a

month ahead of time. When we had made our camp, sometimes we would go away for a day or two, and upon our return, we would find the little wild flowers blooming by our door. Often, now, when we have finished our midday dinner of porterhouse and pie, I sit on the stoop in the sunlight, my faithful dog at my feet, and as I smoke a fifty-cent cigar, my mind wanders back over memory's trail.

I hear the song of brooklets,
The murmurings of the winds;
I smell the smell of summer,
Hear the whispering of the pines.

I seem to see the sunset;
In fancy I behold
The hoary hills above me,
Robed in a garb of gold.

I give an extra cookie
To this dear old dog of mine;
As he shared the shadow,
So shall he share the shine.

And as I smoke and lose me,
In the days that have gone by,
Among the miles of mountains
Beneath a summer sky,

The smoke of my Havanna,
As it slowly floats away,
Is freighted with the odor
Of my long-lost pipe of clay.

And I give an extra cookie
To this poor old dog of mine;
For he has shared the shadow,
And he shall share the shine.

CHAPTER XXI.

NOW let the weary prospector sit down and rest. His dream has been realized; his prophecy fulfilled.

The opening of the Amethyst vein called for the extension of the Denver & Rio Grande Railway Company's track from Wagon Wheel Gap, a distance of ten miles.

About this time, President Moffat and the General Manager got into an entanglement with the directory and both resigned. Mr. George Coppell, chairman of the board, came out from New York and took charge of the property.

Mr. Moffat and others interested,

urged the management to extend the
rails to the new camp. Among those
interested in the extension was Senator
Wolcott, counsel for the company; but
it is as difficult for a New York cap-
italist to appreciate the importance of a
silver camp as it is for him to appreciate the value of a silver dollar, so Mr.
Coppell refused to build the line.

Mr. Moffat then put up thirty-six
thousand dollars to build the extension,
agreeing to let the railroad company
repay him in freight.

Soon after this Mr. E. T. Jeffrey was
elected president and general manager
of the road. Probably no man in
America could have taken up the tools
laid down by Moffat and Smith and continue the good work begun by them,
with so little friction as did the present
president of the Denver & Rio Grande
Railroad Company. To fill the places

vacated by these popular officials was no light task. The grand stand was packed and the voters held the bleachers, when President Jeffrey went to the bat.

Colorado said " Play ball," and in the first inning he won the respect of the other players and the applause of the people. He has been successful because he deserved success.

Three months after the completion of the line to Creede, each train brought to the camp from two hundred to three hundred people, all the side-tracks were blocked with freight and a ceaseless stream of silver was flowing into the treasury of the Denver & Rio Grande Railroad Company. The lucky prospector built a cozy cabin in the new camp and saw a city spring up almost in a day. Just where the trains pulled in, you might see him sitting by the

cottage door, smoking a cigar, while the
little old dog who had just finished a
remarkably good breakfast, trotted stiff-
legged up and down the porch and
wondered why they did n't go out any
more and hunt in the hills.

THE RISE AND FALL OF CREEDE.

A thousand burdened burros filled
   The narrow, winding, wriggling trail.
An hundred settlers came to build
   Each day new houses in the vale.
An hundred gamblers came to feed
On these same settlers—this was Creede.

Slanting Annie, Gambler Joe
   And Robert Ford ; Sapolio—
Or Soapy Smith, as he was known—
   Ran games peculiarly their own ;
And everything was open wide
And men drank absinth on the side.

    *   *   *   *   *

And now the Faro bank is closed,
   And Mr. Faro's gone away
To seek new fields—it is supposed—
   More verdant fields. The gamblers say
The man who worked the shell and ball
Has gone back to the Capital.

The winter winds blow bleak and chill,
  The quaking, quivering aspen waves
About the summit of the hill ;
  Above the unrecorded graves
Where halt, abandoned burros feed
And coyotes call—and this is Creede.

Lone graves ! whose head-boards bear no name,
  Whose silent owners lived like brutes
And died as doggedly, but game,—
  And most of them died in their boots.
We mind among the unwrit names
The man who murdered Jesse James.

We saw him murdered—saw him fall,
  And saw his mad assassin gloat
Above him. Heard his moans and all,
  And saw the shot holes in his throat.
And men moved on and gave no heed
To life or death—and this is Creede.

Slanting Annie, Gambler Joe
  And Missouri Bob are sleeping there ;
But slippery, sly Sapollo,
  Who seems to shun the Golden Stair,
Has turned his time to loftier tricks—
He's doing Denver politics.

CHAPTER XXII.

WEARING HIS WEALTH — ATTRACTS THE
ATTENTION OF ADVENTURESSES — LOS
ANGELES.

TO one who has lived almost alone
and unknown for a half hundred
years, the change from obscurity to notoriety and fame is swift and novel.
Mr. Creede realized that he was attracting the attention of the world, especially
the fair ones in search of husbands, in
a very short time.

In his little den up the Gulch he had
a collection of letters that were interesting reading. They came from the four
corners of the earth; from women of
every tongue, and almost every walk
of life.

The first one I saw was from a
St. Louis play actress, who sent photos
in which her left foot stands at six
o'clock, her right five fifty-five. Her
hair was short and cut curly. She said
she was "dead weary of the stage," and
that with the prospector's money and
her experience, they could double up
and do the world in a way that would
make the swells of "Parie" take to the
woods, and there was nothing the matter with his coming on and she would
meet him on the Q. T., and if she failed
to stack up, he could cash in and quit.

July 11, 1892. A Rhode Island
preacher writes to ask for help.

"Doubtless," he began, " you have many letters
from people upon whom the cares of life press
heavily, and it must be a source of great annoy-
ance."

After dwelling at some length upon
his deplorable condition, there was a—

"P. S.— If you can't send money, please send me a suit of cast-off clothes, and greatly oblige,

Yours truly,

————.

" N. B.— I send measure, so that you can get an idea of what size I need. Breast 37, waist 32, leg 33."

May 17, 1893. A woman with a nose for lucre and a cold nerve, writes from Waxahachie to ask the lucky prospector to " come down and look at her daughter."

" She is a perfect beauty ; has a good solo voice, but is a little lazy. She has not quite developed, being only thirteen years old ; but if you will take a look at her you will change your mind. She's a beauty. She wants to go to Italy or France and study music and if you will help to educate her you may have her."

What a cold-blooded proposition is this, soliciting as a horse trader would for some one who has a fortune to take a look at her child thirteen years oid !

A lady writes from Canada to borrow three thousand dollars to buy a farm, and adds that one man should not have so much money.

An ambitious young Englishman, who is in love with the "prettiest girl in Hold Hengland," writes for a "few 'un-dred to bring 'er hover with."

July 8, 1892, at Columbus, Ohio, a widow writes the best letter of them all.

" DEAR MR. CREEDE :— Having seen by the papers that y's hav lots av money, an' a good disposition I write y's to ask a favor. No it's not money I wants, nor do I want y's to marry me. I was as far west as Colarado wanct, saw the Vergini Mine in Uray County an' its Terrable in 1888. Shure it was terrable, too; for then I lost the best friend av me life — the foreman of the Terrable, he died.

" After that it seemed I had no friends at tall a tall, an' I came back to Columbus. Nearly I forgot to say I was married wanct—but mind, I'm not wan av thim grassy widdies — I'm bonyfied. Shure if I was as shure of another as I am that Pat is dead, shure I wo'n't be wastin' me time writin' to ye. Nearly I forgot to say that what I want av ye is to find me a good thru and 'onest husband. I've lost all fait in these wishy-washy judes here. Gimme the rough and onest hand of the mountain, and take away your long-tinnis judes.

"Comparatively speakin', I was born in the North of Ireland an' am a happy disposition.

"Remembher, the man must be noble, 'onest an' thru. Please write to me soon.

Very respectfully yours,"

———.

"N. B.—After readin' this I see I was about to leave out the most impartent part. Now if you can't find a man with all these good qualities an' money too, I'll take the one wid the 'onest, thru and noble carocther. Money can niver buy happiness an' love, an' that I prize above everything else. I want a man not less than forty as he should begin to have some since by that time.

Wanct more I am,   Yours truly,

———.

Up to the writing of these pages, the mails continue to bring loads of letters from all sorts of cranks. Those from women are turned over to Mrs. Creede; but only a very few, of course, are answered.

In that poet's Paradise; that dreamy lotus-land, Southern California, Creede has bought a beautiful home. It stands just at the end of Sixth street on Pearl, surrounded by tropical trees, vines and flowers. Here the balmy breezes bring down the scent of cedar from the hills to the north, and the soft sea-winds creep across the lea from the ocean-edge. It's a pretty place — a pleasant place for weary pilgrims to rest, beyond the waste of a sun-dried sea —

O'er which he toiled, a sea of sand before him,
Dead snakes and withered toads lay on his way;
The desert sun, red, awful, hanging o'er h m
  The livelong day.

And lo, at last there breaks upon his vision
A paradise with flowers and tropic trees,
Cool, crystal streams that flow throw fields elysian;
  Los Angeles.

CREEDE'S RESIDENCE, LOS ANGELES, CAL.